Jeanne Benameur was born in Algeria to Algerian and Italian parents, who emigrated to France when she was five. She began her writing career with a poetry collection, *Naissance de l'oubli* (1987) and gained popularity with her young adult fiction *Samira des quatre-routes* and *Adil, cœur rebelle*, inspired by her experience as a teacher. She has since become a prolific writer of fiction, non-fiction, poetry and plays, winning multiple national and regional awards such as the UNICEF Prize for her debut novella *Les Demeurées* (The Idiot Women) and the Grand Prix RTL-Lire. Her writings have been translated into many European languages, including Ukrainian and Lithuanian, and several of her works have been adapted for the screen and live music performance. After many years in Paris, she has returned to La Rochelle, where she grew up.

Bill Johnston translates from French and Polish. His most recent translation is Jean Giono's *Ennemonde* (Archipelago Books). His awards include the Best Translated Book Award, the PEN Translation Prize, and the National Translation Award in Poetry.

Praise for *The Child Who*:

'Mystical. A slow hand walking you into
a forest. I come to it to think about loss,
absence and longing, what can never be
ours.'
    – Tice Cin, author of *Keeping the House*

'...driven by reflections on the love between
parent and child and between husband and
wife. And then there's a first-person narrator
who talks to the child directly: "I'd like to
say to you that the world is immense and
lovely, that there's a path for you too."'
    – John Self, *Guardian* Best Recent
                    Translated Fiction

'It's a brief story, but a prodigiously compact
one – the hallmark of all Jeanne Benameur's
books. It's impossible to say enough good
things about her, for the loveliest assessments
will never adequately convey her talent.'
    – Mohammed Aïssaoui, *Le Figaro*

'A work of startling beauty.'
    – Xavier Houssin, *ELLE*

'Aching, tender and luminous, *The Child
Who* explores the splitting of the self that
can occur in response to grief. Finding
beauty even in the most painful dynamics,
this is a humane and moving story touched
by a transcendent lyricism. You will be
haunted by it.'
    – Jessica Traynor, author of *The Quick*

'Jeanne Benameur's work is carved out of silences. Her characters use few words, while she chooses her own with a parsimony that increases their impact tenfold. Suffused in mystery, this novel – about what makes a family, how a personality emerges, how one learns to inhabit the world – is fashioned from a poetry as startling as its title.'
— Raphaëlle Leyris, *Le Monde*

'A marvel.'
— Claire Conruyt, *Le Figaro littéraire*

'For those with the sensibility to respond to its poetic voice, Jeanne Benameur's *L'enfant qui* and the excellent English translation by Bill Johnston have the power to change lives. Existential beyond any philosophical system, the book carefully, lyrically explores the phenomenon of being as it occurs in each of three unnamed family members in an unnamed French village at an unnamed time.'
— Lynn Hoggard

THE CHILD WHO

Jeanne Benameur

Translated from the French
by Bill Johnston

.
LesFugitives

To John Berger,
for the sharing that lives on

In your head of a child there are sudden bright skies wrested from a low, lingering, unfathomable sadness. Your mother has disappeared. Never mind that she was never entirely present, it was her smell, her warmth, her silent hands that you relied on to feel that you truly existed.

Now you get by as you can. Astride a ridge. On one side, your father shouting. On the other, silence. A sheer drop.

From now, your whole life perches on the brink of something that has no name. Your place in the world has contracted. Will it shrink even further? Will you have to reduce yourself to a line, to a single point, in order to stay there at all? You don't yet know the paintings by the Chinese masters, the ink laid down by the brush, barely a stroke, only emptiness besides. If you'd seen them you'd know that now, that is you.

Yet there's your body. Even if you're teaching yourself to breathe while letting the least amount of air possible enter between your ribs. All your bones are there. As long as life is there, they will resist. You can't fight your bones. You sense this failure, and you sense dully, even deeper within yourself, that it was your mother's failure before you.

Stay still, don't be afraid of the abyss. Time will pass. You can rock slowly, gently. Sunlight won't enter the kitchen till midday; until then you can linger in the brightness filtered by the tall trees, with part of the night still about you, calming you. I see you, standing by the window, your gaze elsewhere, or sitting at the table with your little blue bowl in front of you.

You're alone the way someone in a painting can be.

I'd like to lay my hand on your hair. If I close my eyes I can feel its softness, even though no comb can cope with your tangled curls. The palm of my hand grazes against them. You might think it's just a draught blowing through the ill-fitting windows.

You continue your contemplation. A leaf brought all the way to earth by a gust of wind, the dust hovering in the light that reaches right to the corner of your eye. With your fingertip, on the windowpane you follow a path that only you can make out.

The unhurried movement of things calls to you.

And I know that, soundlessly, you're about to set out.

Your grandmother is singing to herself behind the house, in the yard. Your grandmother is always singing, and you like the sound she makes. You let it enter all the way into your chest, as you cling to her hip. Her humming joins with your own breathing, gradually opening up your gaze, your chest of a child. Then you can hear the river flowing far over yonder. Even if everyone says it's impossible to hear the river at such a distance, I know you can hear it. You hold on tight to the apron.

All at once you feel the insistent call. Flee. Quick, quick.

Your feet dash out onto the path and you're gone.

Your grandmother is taken aback. She can no longer feel your head under her arm. You've flown. She'll never manage to notice the exact moment. You leave her standing there, her arms dangling.

It takes her by surprise every time. Jostling in her head are the words Don't be home too late. Where are you going now? Watch out for your father if you come back covered in mud! So many things that have to be said to children. But you.

You're running. You're running. So no eyes should have the time to see you, so your face should not be captured by anyone's gaze. How long has it been since your mother's eyes last rested on you? How long since there's been no mother? The calendar counts in days in months in years. But you, you don't know. You live with only darker moments and brighter moments. In your head, time finds room for itself where it can, the way that space threads its way among the trees in the woods.

Sometimes you lose your mother's face. You haven't yet learned to find it in a faraway icon, near a blue blue sea, looking up tenderly in a painting of the Italian Renaissance. You're thrown into a panic. I hear your breathing. It bumps up against something hard in your chest. You run you struggle against the hard thing in there, a rock. Between your ribs the air is constricted, it whistles. At such times you feel you're still alive. From the pain.

It's a tough method, but it's the only one you have.

Your grandmother's eyes are still turned toward where you disappeared. The words she didn't manage to say to you flutter about her, disperse, find nowhere to settle, go astray. And she's no longer able to return to her chores. She needs a little time to find her head again, as she puts it.

You're already far away.

How can a child like you be protected?

When you come back your father will once again shout What's to be done with him? Eh?

Then he'll bang something on the wooden tabletop, his fist or the tobacco tin, so the sound will continue to resonate after he stops shouting. He needs that. Next he'll mumble some indistinct words, let his rage make a ball of sound closer and closer to his mouth. Then no more. He'll get up, slam the door. The sounds of outside will be enough for him to put away his shouting. When he walks, his silence will weigh heavily.

Where have you fled to?
Will you too be lost, one day?

You stop running only when you hear, right by you, the panting of the dog. The dog always finds you, you don't know how. You've no idea where it comes from. It has no lead, no collar. Quite simply, at a certain moment it's there. It's walking next to you and you sense its presence without even having to look. You don't stroke it right away. You wait. When the dog passes you and sits in the middle of the path, that's the moment.

You drop down to the dog's level, and you stare at it, eye to eye. Time is needed for the dog to enter your head of a child. The second you feel its body quiver, sometimes as lightly as the faintest breath of air, you stand up again. You're no longer alone. And your body no longer weighs you down.

It's not you who strokes the dog, it's the dog that slides its head beneath your hand of a child.

The two of you walk on.

It's as if you were holding hands with someone.

Anyone who saw you, though, would see a child walking all alone, one hand stroking the shadows.

Now your grandmother is watching the clouds as they pass on their strange journeys just above the house.

She breathes in the fresh smell of the laundry that's not completely dry, just right for ironing. She hugs it a little closer to her chest. The freshness of the fabric mingles with the freshness in the crook of her neck, with the journey of the clouds above her. Now they've passed the roof of the house. They move on. She tells herself that she'll do the same, one day.

Your father's calves are heavy from work. He moves heedlessly into the day as it repeats its chores, one by one, the same as always. The child that you are is a puzzle to him. He was unable to keep your mother. She was a stranger. He may not even have wanted to, deep down.

Let her be torn from his life the way she'd entered it, all at once! Let this desire that keeps him caged in be torn out too! Her absence doesn't even set him free. It growls like an animal. The opaqueness of his own desire scares him.

A vagabond, she was. But do vagabonds leave traces? He still has the strange drawing she scribbled before she went away. He's never shown it to anyone. Sometimes, when he's all alone he unfolds it, studies it. Nothing. It's no use turning the paper this way and that. He doesn't understand what she left him. Then, each time he sees once again the moment he met your mother.

One day the lorry driver who delivers

your father's fine cabinetwork to his customers had suggested they ride together along with the latest order as far as a fair in a town some way away, that he'd never even heard of before. He hesitated. But the other man pressed him, and your grandmother nodded her approval. Your father had been too much alone since the death of his fiancée, a nice girl from the village who'd been carried off by a bad sickness the previous winter. Your father had stopped going to dances, to social gatherings. He needed new activities, that's what everyone thought. The lorry driver urged him again. He got in. He spent the whole journey gazing at the changing landscape. The trees were no longer the same.

So that's what fate is? A person climbs into a lorry at dawn after drinking a strong coffee, and sets off. Then, on a market square ten times bigger than anything he's ever seen before, he finds himself in a crowd of people walking this way and that and talking and shouting, slapping each other on the back, fingering the merchandise, sizing up the workmanship, haggling over prices. He was completely bewildered. The lorry driver had gone off on his business. Your father walked around at random. It was a bad idea to come, he was saying to himself. He wasn't used to this.

Fate wore a long faded red skirt, and her hair was pinned up on one side only, as if she hadn't had time to finish the job. She was walking along with others like her, hips swinging slowly, with a bold look in her eye.

Travelling women. Women with no name that can be pronounced. And maybe lives that cannot be pronounced either.

He didn't pull back his hand when she took it, palm upward. The other vagabond women were stopping other people here and there, looking in their hands too and saying things in return for coins. They laughed among themselves or with the people. This woman though: she didn't laugh, she didn't smile. Perhaps that's what fate is, a woman who isn't smiling, who's silent in the midst of all the noise. An island.

The hand of the woman who'd taken his hand, had turned it upwards, it was like touching snow the first few times it falls. Icy and burning. It's impossible to tell one kind of burning from the other. His own hand was trembling. Since the death of his fiancée this was the first time another woman had touched him, and he wanted to run away as fast as possible and he wanted just as much to keep feeling the twin opposing sensations of burning. Two insistent desires at the same time. Was that what it was to be alive? His stomach was aching and he could hear the blood pulsing in his temples. His blood that weighed so heavily. He could rely only on his legs, which were steady, as if they alone were still capable of bringing him back to the safe world of before. But he remained motionless. Like a tree.

For a long time she studied the hardened palm, the hard calloused fingers, their shape fitted for the use of tools. She didn't once raise her eyes to look into his face. And that was good. Her eyes, the colour of dark clouds – he'd discovered them later, when she took him aside, under the trees in a wood, and he'd suddenly smelled the sap and felt a burning sensation, this time inside his belly, his sex, his head. His heart was not bold and had not moved. But his entire body had wanted the woman in the faded red skirt. And that was how she had entered his life. He hadn't made any decision, not at all. It had happened and that was that. He had no explanation to offer. Not to the lorry driver, who asked no questions but stopped making jokes on the return trip, with the woman in the cab next to them, nor to the people in the village who would always move aside as she passed, nor to his own mother. Not to himself.

The shouting had entered the house along with the woman. He'd started to shout, as if at moments his entire being rejected her. Because no, he hadn't chosen her. He'd merely wanted her. Because he understood nothing of this desire that had overcome him, yet he wanted her all the same. Again and again.

As for her, she didn't know the language of these parts and didn't even try to learn it. She kept silent but she stayed. He didn't know why she stayed.

That was how you were born. Torn from your father's shouts and the silence of your mother. In your mother's belly you learned the violence of living.

Since she disappeared you've felt the need to run.

The dog is trotting next to you. No one aside from you can see it, this dog. But you don't know that. Its presence by your side sets my mind at ease. It's strong, and can smell things that you can't see. You can push ahead with your journey. Your woollen top always hangs down on one side, 'you've buttoned Monday with Tuesday,' your grandmother says. You don't entirely understand what that means. It's just that the days no longer know how to follow one another. You're a child who leans. The dog restores the balance.

At times a burst of joy moves through you. You don't know where it comes from. It's the morning lark that finds its rising flight in you. From your feet to your head and much higher than your head, an irrepressible surge lifts you up. There's no reason for the joy. It carries you. And you move forwards.

The dog goes on ahead, runs among the trees, comes back. The dog lives with every blade of grass. Then it sticks its big head under your hand again. You smile.

At such moments you even forget that you're breathing; you're free, so free that a song rises to your throat. To begin with it's like a dull growl. It might sound frightening. Like an animal, perhaps, one unknown to humans. One that had never allowed any sound to reach the air. The sounds were contained in its body, just beneath its skin its plumage its scales, but now are suddenly searching for an exit. Your whole being is quivering from this growl that comes from the earth from roots from everything that life and death have buried so deep and that is rising within you.

You come to a halt. Your breath expands. Your belly your lungs your whole body are ageless now. A song like this cannot be endured by a child's chest. You steady your feet against the earth. Then you stamp on the ground slowly. Right foot. Left foot. Hard. Again. And again. You've seen your mother do this. She would take you into the forest and dance. Your whole body remembers your mother's body and her long faded red skirt. She would spin around. Your mother spins still behind your eyelids.

The rhythm of all those who have breathed on this path on all paths enters through the soles of your feet.

Nothing that has once been human is lost. Ever.

You form one body with the dust of all paths. Your head is a drum resounding from a thousand strong, agile fingers. You tip your head back. Eyes wide open, you see the highest branches of the trees. You see every detail of their leaves as if they were an arm's length away. Your gaze loses itself amid all the greens and then, higher still, the blue of the sky.

Your singing grows in strength.

Your singing relieves you of all gazes all shouting all silences. Your life can join together with any other life. You merge with all that lives all that dies. You're part of it. Time no longer exists.

You're not aware that one day someone heard you. A hunter who was tracking a beast for its skin. At first the hunter thought it was one of those little-known birds that arrive then leave again at the secret signs of the first cold. Birds that had never been seen before were some-times spotted in that region. They were talked about at the Café afterwards.

Your singing brought him to a stop. It was like something calling to the deepest part of him, in a wild, unfamiliar place in his own being. And he was afraid. Afraid in a way that still makes him ashamed today. He thought It isn't human.

Yet he saw that you were merely a child on the path, head tipped back and eyes lost in space. A child all alone in the woods. Singing. He'd recognised the cabinetmaker's son, otherwise he would have thought it was an apparition.

He fled.

What had happened? He'd been thrown into turmoil. He forgot that he was holding a gun that he was tracking a beast which had almost been within range. His dog pressed silently against his leg. Its coat had bristled as if another, more powerful animal had been near, but it hadn't growled. It had only pressed against the hunter's leg, forming a single body with everything that within it was bending gently toward the earth, meeting roots and entrails of beasts and men far, far down.

The hunter had turned around, disappeared toward the village.

That evening he'd wanted to tell his wife about it, in the darkness of their warm bed. But something held back his voice. A sense of shame that was at once profound and sweet, like we have as children when confronted with the proof of what we will never attain, when we feel that the dreams of the world are much too huge for us to carry them on our heads. That we'll never manage it. For certain. And that deep inside we know our parents couldn't carry them either, nor our parents' parents, and so it goes on this earth.

But you, you carried everything on your head. Alone. Because without knowing it you'd come to terms with all the darkness beneath your feet.

The man has never spoken of it but sometimes, at night, when he's unable to enter into sleep, he again hears your singing deep inside himself.

I see you. You're in front of me, on the path. I follow you. You're walking like someone who knows the road and who cannot be stopped by anything. Yet I'm aware that you have no idea where your steps are taking you, but that you need to turn your back on all that is too oppressive in the house, all that prevents you from living.

After your singing, you have unexpected strength in your legs. No one ever would have suspected that on such little legs it was possible to go so far.

You forget the time for soup, and all the other times of the village. The branches of the trees shake them till they come loose and float away, clinging to the feathers of birds. You raise your head and for as long as you can, with your eyes you follow the powerful flight of grey and blue flecks above the trees. The times will fall into unknown seas when the birds spread their wings on their long journey.

While you, in your legs you have the

strength of all the steps your mother has stopped taking. Your body is so light that your legs could fold up. You too could fly. House school village, all would disappear. Only your mother's crazy spinning remains in you.

When you walk for such a long time, you notice every sound made by the forest. Your ears, washed clean of all words, hear the rustlings the hidden murmurs the shifting of shadows. You grasp the mystery of noises that no human creates. They are sounds that are tangled together, sometimes one muffles another for a time, but even the faintest, the frailest, appears again distinctly.

In the world you're walking in, every sound has its place.

You close your eyes. Your singing has carried even your name away from you.

There remains your bare, fresh skin. Your hearing that is utterly new. Perfect.

Now you can hear like the dog. You're part of the world of the forest.

Your mother said to you one day that all those who walk on paths are trees. Afterwards the earth can do whatever it wishes with them, it no longer matters. Those who walk on paths already belong in their innermost being to that which does not move. If they walk, it's only because human beings have legs. Like them, you walk. But the strength in your legs is that of everything beneath the earth, that which waters the roots of the trees, which abide where they are.

You gaze at them, head raised. The great flights of birds have passed.

You believe in that immobility rising directly all the way to the sky.

Now you feel the bark beneath your fingers. You're pressing against an oak that looks as if it's guarding the nearby space. A tree like a door, that opens and protects at the same time. You wrap your arms around it. They're too short to reach all the way. Still, your chest is broad, as broad as that of any adventurer who walks all the way to the innermost depths of his heart.

Your cheek against the bark of the tree, you smell the mixed scents of what grows of what breathes like you. The scents are intermingled, like the sounds. A mesh. But little by little you tell them apart. You perceive the lush smell of an unfamiliar plant. A fainter odour of something approaching with small fearful steps. An animal that knows its fragile animal existence, that is alert, its only defence its noiselessness and its speed. You sense the slightly sour, hot smell of its fear and you wish you could tell it not to fear anything from you. But the terror of defenceless animals is the ancient terror of humans; it is very ancient indeed, and nothing can be done about it. It returns when the fury of people against other people comes, attacking, laying waste.

In the world far from the forest you know that there are sometimes wars. The word has lodged in your chest like the hot sour fear in the blood of the small animal. But you, you never wanted to play that game with the village children.

War is a word that is hard as stone.

One day, in the forest you saw a tramp walking along barefoot. His feet were grey with dust, covered with strong wrinkled skin like that of elephants. You remembered the day when you and your mother had lingered in front of a poster put up in the village. On the poster there were animals, a circus was passing through. You held her hand tightly in your own. You were afraid she would leave, called by another life that was too strong, that was barely contained by the colours of the poster. You asked the name of those powerful grey creatures. To bring her back to you, her child. Elephant remained in a corner of your memory. Elephant says gray, and the weight of days of slow walking. Elephant says it's possible to move forwards step by step, without knowing where the way is leading. It's a comforting word in a child's life. The man in the forest felt neither thorns nor pebbles beneath his elephantlike feet. He nudged aside a heavy rock, the kind you skirt around when you're walking. The man had pushed it to the edge of the path with a single movement of his bare foot. Just like that.

You think about war the way you think about that rock. Heavy hard. But an unarmed man a man with nothing but life on his shoulders could push it aside with only the foot that was carrying him on his long march.

You wonder whether your singing could also shift something in the world, like the foot of the elephant.

Now that you hear everything, that you smell everything, like the dog, your skin becomes fur. Protected from any word any thing that might try to make of you what you are not.

Your mouth of a child is a cave. The words are there, deep inside.

Everyone keeps repeating that you can talk when you want to but you don't want to. Like your mother. Your father conceals all misfortunes with his voice. But it's air. Nothing but air. Whereas the misfortune of your mother was a rock. Hard. Very hard. And it could not be rolled.

You wave your hand in front of your mouth, in front of your eyes, you chase images away. You need to keep walking. Until your head is empty.

When you reach the place in yourself and in the forest that forms a kind of cross, outside and inside join together again. When you reach there, at the heart of that invisible crossing you feel that you are alive. At last. Whatever comes into your head is yours. Yours alone. Nothing of the muddled and unhappy world of the house mingles with it any more.

From there, you would have a great power of speech. Your words would come out and perhaps, with your foot of a child you would roll the rock of your mother's sadness far aside.

But your mother has disappeared. People said, The Woman Who Disappeared.

No one ever knows how to lighten the sadness of mothers who disappear. Sadness itself does not disappear.

Every day your father goes to the Café in the village. He waits for the day to end, in the room where the proprietor and his wife usually eat, where the smell of their meal mingles with that of the footsteps of everyone who comes and goes, passes through the door, sits for a while, then leaves again. The Café is a warm place that has no stories other than those of the lives of the village that everyone knows, that do not need to be told. The life of one person, the life of another, side by side at the table. Words that make just enough noise for them to feel they're alive, they're together. They could be speaking Chinese, it would make no difference. Tiredness eases its hold on legs on arms on backs. Never to the point of weakening. They have to be able to rise to their feet again. Heads hang down. If they weren't careful, eyelids might sometimes droop.

Life gnaws away at him, but here he finds respite. It's the moment in the day that he likes the best. And so what if the wine is too heavy in his head when he goes back and shouts some more, he no longer knows why. In the end he'll go to sleep in his cold bed.

How can someone go, just like that, leaving nothing but a drawing behind? There are those who say she's been seen far away, on another square, at another fair, but your grandmother said You mustn't listen to them, she's gone and that's that.

So he takes out the drawing, studies it for a long time by the window in the dark dark night. Nothing.

In the forest now you're sitting at the foot of a tree.

At this moment you feel you could enter into the secret of your mother's words. The words that she held back with her fine jaw. Like birds of unimaginable plumage beating against her closed teeth. Nestling in the roof of her mouth so close to her throat. The slightest thing and they would slip back down into the depths. So that by the time she unclenched the so- delicate bones of her jaw, it was too late.

For your mother, it had always been too late.

She choked back her troubles, choked back her anger. All that remained was shame, like fog in the mouth. A cottony wad of shame stuck to her gums.

You – when you're alone deep in the woods, you could do it.

And it doesn't matter that your mother is so far away nothing remains of her anywhere. You close your eyes. You think of touching her throat with your fingertips, touching her closed lips. Only then.

Leaning back against her absence, you set out on your perilous journey.

You curl up in your closed mouth. You roll with the swallowed words. They're there. Hardened resonant held back. Like iron-grey clouds right before the dense rains of spring come bursting.

They wait.

You – you believe in dust.

You believe in the shade of trees.

Prayers prayers. Roots that will never see snow, that know only the dark weight of the earth.

You believe in the dark weight of the earth.

Birds are lucky. All the shouting in the world beneath their wings doesn't stop them from flying. You – you do not fly.

You do not try to work out where the dog that no one can see is leading you. You know he'll guide you even if night has fallen by the time you go back. Sometimes you think Go back? Why?

You move forward blindly. The lower branches obstruct your view. It doesn't matter. You hold them aside with your hands just enough for your body to pass. Wherever the dog can get through, you can too.

The dog never barks, never growls. But its silence is not the same as that of the trees. It's a silence that moves in the air. The silence of fur.

It has stopped all of a sudden.

It's standing in front of something, motionless. It looks like a statue of a dog.

There's a sort of mist that prevents you from seeing. You stop too, the silence of fur beneath your hand.

In front of you is some kind of very old house.

You see the façade of crumbling grey wood. You make out windows. There are no curtains and you can't tell if there are any panes left.

This house has been eaten away by time.

No one could live in it.

No story could remain in it.

It's just a place put there. Off the path.

There's no garden to make it clear to anyone that they've left the forest and come to a place made by people. The forest has consumed the space right up to the threshold of the house.

Now you're in front of the door. With your fingertip you push on the wooden panel. Nothing resists any more.

The stone of the threshold is so worn it barely still marks the entryway.

Inside, leaves have come in, driven by one autumn after another. Dry now, they form a carpet of fine dust. There are no longer any true colours.

Everything is hazy. You have to blink, sharpen your sight.

The dog stays outside. It waits by the door. Maybe it smells old scents. Maybe it sees old things in its doggy head.

You walk in the house's only room.

You sit down at the table, lean your elbows on the wooden top, cup your chin in the palm of your hand. You look around closely. This is your kingdom. What you see has not been used for many years. Useful objects that are no longer used become strange. Their life is slower. You see that life. You find it restful. No hand now has touched this furniture in passing, opened a drawer, picked up a teacup, or heated water in the pot. But it's all there. You see the emptiness between each thing. It is silence. Here everything is asleep like in your grandmother's stories but there's no princess to wake up from the spell. While you – you're too small to be a prince.

You're nothing but a child of brambles and dust. You like the timeworn house.

You swing your legs slowly, the tips of your feet graze the floor each time they pass. I see the mark they leave.

Little by little kitchen activities come back to you. In front of everything that is no longer used, here, you can gently place your mother. Bringing to mind the movements surrounding the evening meal, your breakfast bowl in the morning, the rustle of her long skirts, you rock yourself.

Now the words hiding in your mouth come back. They stir between your ribs. You place a hand on your child's chest.

The words are powerful.

And it's as if a heavy wave coming from afar were lifting you. It surges all through your head, sweeping everything up as it goes. The timeworn house floats on the powerful current that is now swirling in your blood, rushing, mingling sky and earth. Everything pitches and rolls. East west south north. Your mother's footsteps have gone astray. Perhaps she placed her confused foot here. Her footprints have been covered by the dust from the rotting leaves. Your mother's steps are no longer anywhere at all.

You've curled up in the hollow of the old hearth. You hold your thin arms tight against yourself. From there it's as if you're in the hold of a ship battling against the storm. Eyes closed, you let your memory be tossed by the swell.

Then your mouth opens. Your breath shapes sounds. I am the only one that hears them. I lean toward you, close to your mouth. It's an unknown language. The secret language of your mother. The one in which she spoke to you in the safety of the forest. The words are there. Tattooed beneath your skin. Your body huddles around your memory. Every word launched into the air by your mother's voice is inscribed in your bones.

You clench your fists. To hold in the blood the life that might fly away with the words, there's no telling.

Maybe people disappear for having spoken the words. Even if they weren't talking to anyone. If they only said them to the stones. Even if it was only in the silence of their heads.

These questions and the very old fear form a swirling mist in your body. Your mother's language rises in a cloud like the dry leaves. You have nothing left of her but the words. Nothing but the words. Yet they're there. And no one, no one can wipe them away. Your memory is yours. Yours alone. Your father and his shouting can do nothing. Your mother's language is there. In you. That is your secret.

Now the powerful wave ebbs. You remain, bathed in silence.

Your face suddenly looks very old.

I think that you are like the objects no one handles any more. And like the space between the objects. That's of no consequence. It's your own life. You walk unhurriedly out of the house of mist and dry leaves. The dog comes and places its head under your hand. You do not close the door.

The dog sets off. You follow behind. When you look back there is nothing now but a tangle of branches and mist. A house?

Your father knows nothing of women who are dead. He ought to. To understand something of his own life. His old mother is alive but she cannot teach him about them. Mothers who are still alive can't be asked to explain women who are dead. That isn't the way things are. A person works hard, goes to the Café with the others, they do everyday things and they ask no questions. They can't. What would such a thing mean.

This man, your father, is alive. Between two women who are dead. First his fiancée from the village, then your mother. For the first one he can go to the cemetery. For the other he can't, since her body is nowhere. No white hairs appear yet on your father's head. One day he'll have some, like the old people in the village, and he'll remember that he was the man who lived between two women who were dead. One under the ground. The other not. Is it easier when you have white hairs.

He looks at his hands. Your mother never told him what she had read in them. Maybe her disappearance was already there, amongst the clear lines of his palm. That's what he tells himself. Maybe she already knew everything when she followed him. Why then? Why this scrap of life. A few years snatched from what?

He slides his palms slowly down his jacket then his trousers of thick fabric, as if he were wiping dirty water off his hands. In fact they're dry. Yet he repeats the motion, slowly, pressing hard. He feels his body under his work clothes. His everyday body. Under everyday fabrics. This same body, in the night, is despair. All alone for so long now. He won't go anywhere to look for another woman. That's over.

He saw the fields of rapeseed this morning. Their intense light, that seemed to come from the earth instead of the sky. And the colour choked him with emotion. There it was. The yellow of the rapeseed, filled with life. And him with his hard belly. Never touching the belly of a woman again. Clouds passed over his head in profound indifference. He is nothing. Nothing in this world. This morning he feels it so strongly.

It had been no use telling him that women like that cannot be kept. He'd believed in her dark eyes, in her hips that had fitted so well between his hands, her back that had pressed her whole belly against his. In her deep, soft sex. He'd believed in the nameless mystery of legs that opened in the night. She held him so tight against herself. He can still feel her hands on his back if he lets himself go to the memory of the occupied bed. She holds him, and her black hair is soft as soft on his neck. He passes his rough fingers over her skin. He can feel the light, light softness of her hair. She says things he does not understand. But he doesn't want to hear the words of that language. He doesn't understand why but they frighten him. The unknown sounds prevent him from grasping the soul of the woman. He puts his hand over her mouth. Sometimes she weeps.

The man can no longer stay in place when memory is in his hands, beneath his skin, atremble. He walks, taking long strides. At the Café he'll find the others. And if it's too early to stop work, so what. Because his whole body can no longer stand this memory that comes back so powerfully. He'll drink the cheap wine and gradually feel everything be doused in his veins. That's what it is: all that he feels coming and sweeping him away needs to be doused. He'll lay his head on his numb arms. He'll feel himself being overcome by torpor. He'll forget the haziness of the unfamiliar words. The other people will not wake him. They know that if they do, he's going to shout. Loud. The others will act as if he were sleeping because the day had begun too early, a hard day filled with work, that's what they'll say. The others know how to do what's needed with a man who can no longer bear his dreams. The village is able to protect itself. Who knows what dream could impose itself on everyone like an ill-intentioned guest if one of their number were allowed to open his mouth and shout the bad dreams of life. The village's large body is vigilant. And he is a member of the village. He's learned to lean on it like his father before him, and his father's father.

The Café is a reliable refuge. Your mother never once set foot in there.

On this day, his head cradled in his arms, he dreams he's wearing big boots and that in his boots are his tools and all his life marching with him. But he doesn't know where he is going.

In the dream, someone passes a hand

across his forehead. He feels someone's skin against his skin.

The owner's wife has just placed a bowl of hot soup in front of him. The fragrant steam warms the air close to his face. He wakes up, sluggish from the sounds all around him. It's hard for him to leave the boots from the dream. He picks up the bowl of soup and lifts it to his lips, not knowing if he's at home or elsewhere. It's some time before the voices of the others properly wake him.

Once night has fallen he leaves, in a strange state. He wishes he could go back into his dream and walk for a long time with all his life in his boots.

While you – you've always found it hard to live in the rooms of the house. Everything that ought to be your familiar world is strange to you. Even your small bedroom at the end of the hallway.

You've never been able to think 'my house'.

You've never been able to inhabit it.

How to make it clear that you're like a bird at the edge of its nest? that there's no place that is yours? that there is no house? Your mother knew this. She knew it in her snowbound body. The two of you, you did not inhabit any place. Only the breath that came out of your mouths.

You remember her smell. When she comes back to you, your blood courses in your body. That smell – yes, you inhabited that, and the fabric of her skirts, and the amber colour of her skin.

But it isn't possible to inhabit a person. Once in the world, we have to inhabit the world. People say she left you 'alone in the world'. You've heard this and you're trying to grasp it. Alone means without her, that much you understand. But the world… the world is too immense. Even if you're capable of walking far, very far, on your small tireless legs. I'd like to teach you, to say to you that the world is immense and lovely, that there's a path for you too. One day, in a big city, elsewhere, far away, you'll see a little painting that will say all that. It shows a man walking alone with his dog. In the snow. In the distance is what may be a house, a simple red mark. And there's so much solitude and so much hope in the steps of that man. I gazed at it for a long time. You, you keep your eyes wide open in the darkness of your room. You are the origin of my solitude.

When your mother was still there, you would take her hand and study all the lines on the inside.

Was that where your only house was?

Do the lines traced on the palms of mothers depict the only house we can inhabit?

She would relinquish her hands to you. Her eyes would be looking into the distance. In her open palm you would try to decipher the strange patterns, perhaps distant lands, cities that could barely be made out, between rock and sand.

You did not dare ask her what it was she herself saw at such times. A furrow would form on your forehead, a narrow channel by which to recall your mother's eyes to you. But she would not come back.

The open hands of mothers are picture books.

And childhood teaches concern for life that is lost.

Most often, in the night of the house you are unable to reconcile yourself to either the time or the space that you have to share with others.

You are truly alone.

It's no use striving to be as present as you can so as to act like them, at table; you quickly become once more a snowman being melted by the sun. All the tiny crystals of cold that keep you upright break apart. All that's left is a little scrap incapable of saying the words with the others.

You have nowhere to live in that world.

I'm well aware that you need to make yourself tiny, even tinier, a speck of dust of a little boy, in order to find within yourself a place to stand. Will even that place disappear too one day?

Luckily you have the dog that no one

can see and the houses it takes you to. You can go back there in your head.

I know that often, you wait for the night. Other children like to remain in the glow of lamps and the murmur of evening voices. Not you.

Inhabiting the night, in your little bed, is easier. No one is watching you. You let your eyes wander across the dim shapes looming in the semi-darkness. The indistinct shapes are your friends. You call them silently. In the shadows of the room you see tall trees and things you do not recognise. You like to see women squatting around a dark fire, saying nothing, calm, minding the fire that does not give off any light.

Their presence in the blackness soothes you. It's often then that you fall softly asleep.

In your dreams there is singing that responds to your mother's singing. Voices from a great fire, forests lit up. In your dreams your mother does not show herself but you sense her. Everywhere.

You do not like coming back in the morning. You keep your eyelids firmly shut, even if you're awake. You don't move. Your grandmother comes and speaks of the day that is waiting for you, as she opens the shutters. But you know full well that the day is not waiting for you. The day does not wait for anyone.

Still, you have to get up.

If there were no dog, you'd no longer be living at all.

This is a strange day. Yesterday you heard your father's heavy steps coming back from the Café, very late, later than usual.

In your ear are muffled rhythms that have come from the night, while powerful yet blurred images are behind your neck when you open your eyes.

It's dawn and no one in the house is awake yet. You sit up abruptly and get out of bed. I can make you out as you stand in the semi-darkness, and I'd like to tell you that it's too early, that at this time children are still asleep and waiting for the daytime. But you – you're listening to the sleeping house. A particular kind of silence. Not the same as when the house is empty. It's the silence of hazy breathings. You like this kind of silence.

When you open the door the day is still wrapped in the milky shadow of night. Outside it looks as though the brightness were fraying, whereas in fact it's taking shape. The beginning and the end are alike. You too, not long ago, were still in the milky night of your mother's belly. One day you'll be in that slow mist again, and that will be the end. Between the two will have been your whole life.

Such things drift without words in the special silence of this morning, I'm certain that they enter into your head of a child because children think far. I see your fingers on the handle of the door. You close it softly behind you.

You reach out toward the mist, as if to take a handful of it. That's how it is, you say out loud. Your voice in the mist makes a light, very precise wave. Anyone who were to hear you at this moment would know that your articulation is clear and your voice melodious. You repeat the words. You like that expression, one of those your grandmother uses. And depending on what she's talking about, it's either light or very heavy. That's how it is, you say again as you move down the path. That's how it is. You repeat the words till they lose their meaning, till they become no more than a cadence accompanying your steps.

The dog appeared suddenly at the moment you launched those words into the dawn. It laps at the mist. At the words too. Do words speak a secret language in the heads of dogs? Its coat is wet as though it had just been in the river. But it may just be the night leaving dark droplets on its fur.

You clap the palms of your hands against one another then rub them till warmth reaches every part of your body. No part of you should remain trapped in the ice of past days. You hop from one foot to the other, someone might think you're playing or trying to dance. But no.

You're just attempting to remain alive between the beginning and the end.

It's your own way of deferring the end when it sticks too much to the daylight. If you were familiar with the rites of other countries far away, you'd know that from the beginning of time humans have done what you are doing this morning, so as to defer death. The slap of their bare feet against the earth pushes them into the world of the living when death comes too close.

In today's cities they've come up with other ways. They sit and listen to music, or contemplate things painted by those like them; still others read books. They have a thousand ways. While you – all you have is what your mother's bare feet taught you. Perhaps one day it will no longer be enough for you. Perhaps one day you'll need to invent a way that is yours alone. But today, it's enough for you to feel the ground that you strike with your foot tremble all the way up to your knees. At that moment the weight of the things that live under the earth, in the secrecy of tangled roots and rocks that cannot be rolled aside by any foot, falls back into its rightful place.

You are still at the beginning, at the very beginning. You need to go on for a long time yet. Alone.

As long as mothers walk alongside us, we don't have to worry about knowing the way. We walk in the innocence of our own footsteps.

You though, you lost that innocence very early. Perhaps that's what a destiny is.

On this morning, the dog that no one sees does not stray from the way. It walks without the least glance either at you or at anything around it. Its gait is magnetic.

The two of you quickly reach the forest. The dog abruptly turns off where there is no path at all. You follow. Your heart is beating. The blurred images from the night come back and surround you. Their indistinct colours cloak you. Your slim fingers find the strength needed to push aside a heavy branch, then another. Your fingers on the bark of the trees are now the only human signs that your eye can fix upon. If it weren't for seeing your own hand you could forget that you exist. The compactness of the forest is so much more powerful than that of a human being. You hear your own breathing and the sound reassures you. Your breathing is not that of the animals of the forest, nor that of the dog. It really is that of a human.

You are the only human in the forest.

The dog moves forward soundlessly. Now you place your hand on the dark fur. To touch that fur is to feel that time comes from very far away. Beneath your hand, that which is distant. In your mother's eyes, that which is distant. And also in the compactness of the forest, and in its smell. That which is distant is everywhere. Must you disappear into it.

It is then that a new house appears. Just behind the tall trees. There is no path any more. Only a passageway like a wrinkle between knotty, close-set trunks. Your body catches on the bark of the trees. Is held back. Your jacket is torn. You make it through.

The house is brown. Walls that are still standing and, in the middle, a hollow.

The door is gone. The hole is round, almost perfectly formed. A person could slip inside and stay there, with the high walls all around. Instinctively you rest your foot on the tumbled stones. Your hand lingers on the walls covered with shadows and lichen.

Now the dog begins to walk around the outside of the house as if around a wheel. It doesn't look at anything. Its feet have a slow, regular rhythm. It's showing something with its almost perfect circles. But nothing occurs to your dulled mind. You scramble across to the other side of the hollow. Your little body standing at its full height, on a terrace with no guardrail you receive the rising light full in the face. You lean over. Down below is the dog with its nearly perfect circles. You follow its movements gravely with your eyes. The dog is a good master. You decide to do what the dog is doing. So as to understand. In your turn you walk around the hollow, taking care not to slip. In your turn, with slow regular steps you make nearly perfect circles.

You walk around like the dog is doing. In your head of a child there is nothing but the dog's footsteps. This goes on a long time. And then – after how long?

– your memory gives back to you, like a treasure, a strip of fabric decorated with tiny red beads. You see this curious bracelet once again. It's on your mother's wrist. It's an almost perfect circle. You remember your mother's delicate bones beneath your fingers and how you liked to feel them under the beads. Each bead was a little bulge, a hard teardrop. Your mother's sorrow all around her wrist, hard as the pebbles of the path.

You know the story of the bracelet. It came from another time, was worn on other wrists. Always by women. Always by those who looked at lives in the palms of other people.

She said One day it'll be taken from my wrist too and it'll go to someone else.

You continue circling the hollow and your mother's bracelet occupies your head. It was too big for your wrist. Too small to go around your waist.

You see again the large bead that fastened it. How it reflected the light. Around whose wrist are your mother's red teardrops today?

The birds are there. You hear them without seeing them. The birds know everything about the women who walk the roads and about those that disappear. Amid the stones their song does not resonate the way it does in the branches of the trees. It becomes mineral.

You stop walking around the imprint of the house. You sit at the edge of the broad hole. The sun is high in the sky. The heat strikes your head, enters into the stones. You could let sleep come. The house would close around you like a shell and the sounds of the forest would gradually soften. Is that how mothers disappear?

Beneath the stones, you say to yourself that your mother's words are kept next to the earth. You hear the murmur of the secret language rising from the buried roots. The stones should be lifted up. One by one. So air can get in, and the broad daylight of the open road. But there are so many stones. You can't lift all of them. Your life would not be long enough. So then, at the edge of the broad hole you listen. In your head the voice of your mother. It too is mineral.

The words are unknown.

It's a language of the underside of things.

The language of your mother's body.

A language that had moved beneath the feet of all those who walk the roads, in their blood, beneath their skin and beneath the stones.

The language is old and dark. You hear it. It speaks the inside and the outside, the skin between them. Delicate. Alive.

It labours.

The grammar of that language is not learned anywhere. No one can teach it. It's an untamed language. Which travels from body to body, can only be passed on through the silence of the skin. A language that is blind in the manner of a little one nestling in its mother's belly, not yet delivered into the world. It's the language of muted dreams and the myths of humans. Some people never know it throughout their lives. Others let it come sometimes, in love or in silence, returning from the secrecy of their memory. It was this language alone that your mother spoke. You, in her belly, you heard it. Your memory quivers.

To dare to go to the very depths of the earth.

To make that language yours.

To dare.

You let your little legs slide over the rocks over the earth. Your whole body follows. You do not shout, do not call for help, you let your body tumble like the stones in the hollow. You too are a stone. Right at the bottom, all the way down.

The sky so far away.

There's only room for one single body. Only one. Yours.

Your eyes are wide open and the sky is vast.

There are moments in life when everything can be understood. The manifestness of birth, of unseeing links woven by body and blood. Every mouth that opens on nothing. Nothing but air. That enters, lays out a nameless memory, sets aquiver all that does not know itself and is life.

It is this kind of moment that you are living. Few people on earth experience it so early. You do. You understand. You understand and you weep. You understand that you are alone. Through your entire being. And it's different than hearing it in the words of others. You understand that your mother will never be there again, her reassuring body between you and the world. You say aloud Never again. The earth hears you. The stones hear you. She does not. She can no longer hear or see anything, and her hands are useless, and her feet are turned elsewhere.

Never again.

These two words are yours from now on. There's nothing more to know. But you are able to understand everything. Understand the blackness and dimness of the earth. Understand that bones go missing, that one day nothing is left but their naked whiteness and that that does not make light. Understand the dust.

Look at the palms of your hands. No story is traced on your skin. There is no voice to invent a life for you. But you have language and it is at work. You've not looked for anything but that's how it is. It's your own life. I wish I could take you in my arms and tell you not to be afraid.

Now, for the first time the dog lets its voice be heard. It breathes out a long, long sound and you realise that the dog is howling its 'Never again'. For you. For your disappeared mother. That the two words make a long howl in its doggy throat.

Now you too, from the depths of the earth, you can howl.

Your mouth wide open. I hear you.

The howling of the dog the howling of the child, there is nothing else besides in the world of the forest.

The birds have fallen quiet. The trees stand there silently. The howling raises leaves branches feathers bark. A mighty breath. Perhaps it reaches even further, to the world of houses.

At this moment you have to climb back up to the daylight. To clutch at earth at roots and haul yourself up. Go. The dog is waiting for you. Take hold of its heavy fur. The dog is the only help you have, and what does it matter that no one can see it. It's there for you alone.

Stand on your feet again.

This day is strange for your father too. He woke late. He's not in the habit of sleeping so long. He had dreams but does not recall any images, only the feeling of his heavy head, though not the way it is after wine.

It's the day of the week when your grandmother leaves early on her 'rounds'. From farm to farm, she buys everything the three of you need to live. You yourselves grow no vegetables, raise no animals.

The house is empty.

Your father heats up some black coffee, and because he's alone in the house and he isn't used to it, something unfamiliar comes over him, a slowness in his movements, a kind of silence of his entire body. It's as if sleep has not properly left him. He tries to chase away the strangeness of this sensation: a still-sleeping body inside his own body. But nothing can be done, the feeling persists. He pours more coffee, which is very hot, slowly breathes in the bitter smell. His eyelids close.

He finds himself back in the times

when he was a child, right here. In this kitchen that the coming of a woman did not alter, where only the motions of childhood remain. Your mother left no trace here. And for the first time, he finds that strange. As if nothing of his life had happened to him.

He drinks the coffee. He knows this taste well. But saying it to himself, this morning, causes him to feel different inside. As if he were watching his own life, his routine, from a distance that renders things strange and visible. An unfamiliar compactness is making his world opaque, and he wishes to chase that away too. He senses a rising anxiety of which he is not the master. He tries a blow with the flat of his hand on the tabletop as if to say That's enough! It produces a loud bang the way he knows how to do it. A noise that ordinarily makes heads duck like turtles pulling back into their shells. He tries a cuss word, but his own voice and the sound of the word seem strange too because no one is there to hear them. No one but him.

As a child, whenever he was truly afraid of something he would get over it by whittling sticks. Where did those great fears of childhood come from, and the fear that has come back today – what is it made of? He has never asked such questions. But today his memory prowls insistently.

In his father's workshop, at the end of the yard, was what everyone called the 'lodge'. A kind of lean-to where unwanted things were kept. Old tools, crates, chairs that needed reseating. As a child he would slip into the lodge. He liked the acrid yet at the same time sweetish plant-like smell of old rotting wood. What your grandmother called the 'stink' kept him safe from her visits. Today his memory continues its work in the empty kitchen. One day, he recalls, he had picked up some tree branches blown down by a fierce wind. It was in the spring, when April goes from sunshine to strong winds, then to sudden heavy showers. During a break in the clouds he had gathered some fallen wood and taken it to the lodge. And never mind the wind and the rain squalls, his hands were craving work.

In the house it was his mother's hands that he always saw occupied. Those of his father rested flat on his thighs when he came back and waited for dinner.

He remembers that he envied the hands of the women because in the house they never stopped touching different things all day long. Soft warm wool and the thin metal of needles; the smooth, always slightly damp and slippery touch of the vegetables they peeled; the clothes they washed, and the earthenware, and the wood of the furniture they waxed. Every evening those hands were rich with all they had felt. An entire living world in the crook of their palms. Whereas he, in the house, was forbidden to touch most things. He did it anyway, surreptitiously. But he took all the time he wanted to observe; that was what had enabled him to become the good cabinet-maker that he was.

This morning, in the kitchen, he realises that in every woman he has met, it's always the hands he looks at first.

As for your mother, she never gave him the time to do so. At the fairground she was the one who took hold of his hand first. He didn't have time. Perhaps that is what destiny is.

Time passes and he's still sitting at the kitchen table. His memory is not letting go of him. He sees himself when he was small, the bundle of wood in his arms, pushing open the door of the lodge with his foot, ready to make up motions that cause a person to belong to the world. His hands of a child have stripped the branches of their leaves, they've returned each one to its original form, which the springtime conceals under foliage in the space of a few days. He felt happy, truly, to hold a branch in his hand, nice and firmly, and to go all the way to smooth bare wood. His father had given him a knife for Christmas. He hadn't used it much yet. He took it out of his pocket and began to scrape off the bark. He made incisions with the point of the blade and whole pieces of bark came away beneath his fingers. He had liked that.

Now I see his hand pushing back the coffee cup on the tabletop. He still has the knife. He takes it out from deep in his pocket, lays it flat on the table. It has followed him everywhere. It's with this knife that he wants to do something today.

He stands up. Goes out.

How long is it since he last crossed the threshold of the lodge? He breathes a deep sigh. There are days in life when it isn't clear what direction time is flowing in. Perhaps that too is destiny. Simply obeying the desire of his hands, he enters the lodge. Light comes in through the skylight. It filters sievelike through the dust, making everything look strange. His heart is heavy. He no longer feels at ease here. He's too big, he has to lower his head so as not to bump it against the sloping ceiling. He rights the stool on which he used to perch, instinctively wedges its one shorter foot on the uneven floor the way he used to, to make it level. Performing this action from before sets the rest in motion. As then, he sits, rests his elbows on the bench. Now he would need a branch to whittle. But his hands are empty. He has nothing but memories, and he's no desire to peel away their bark. Still, he takes out his knife and holds it in his hand. Feeling the handle snug in his palm, back in this place again, reassures him and troubles him at the same time. What is he looking for here? There's no answer to what is gnawing away at him. Your mother has disappeared. People say she's dead. People don't know anything. No one knows anything. There is no body.

All of a sudden he needs air and light to come in. It's a pressing want. He fights with the skylight, which resists. He leans all his strength into it. When he succeeds, he's braced against it so hard that he loses his balance and barely manages to recover. A splinter enters deep under his skin. With the point of his knife he draws out the needle-thin piece of wood, then he makes the blood flow to clean it. The thought that his fingers have become branches, that there's nothing left but to strip them of bark. He applies the blade of the knife to the palm of his hand. It would be enough to make a couple of cuts and all the lines of his hand would be muddled up. His life with them. It would have to be remade. But he no longer has the strength for new beginnings. It's over. He presses on the tip of his finger till the bleeding stops completely. Then he leaves the lodge, exhausted by something that is unfamiliar to him. Today he won't break free from his memory.

He does not turn back toward the house. He walks, his head heavy with a stubborn memory.

On the branches, he remembers, he left rings of bark. He carved signs in them. He remembers too that he was proud because the signs looked like letters even though he didn't yet know how to write. A whole alphabet made up with the tip of the knife. It didn't look like any language. Your mother, perhaps, would have been able to decipher it. He never told her about all that. So many things that people don't say. And today. He touches the crumpled drawing that he slipped into his pocket this morning. People do things sometimes... would anyone be able to teach him to understand that? What do people learn in a life? Who teaches what it means to live? And to disappear.

The tips of your fingers brush against the bark of the trees. You still have the warm feeling of the earth against your belly. You crawled out of the house with the hollow, it was like leaving a tunnel. The dizziness of the circling is still in your head. You've become a spinning question in the world.

You are a tiny wheel in the universe

You say words in a language you do not know. The untamed language of your mother in your mouth. You send the sounds one by one into the forest. Forests are made for that. Forests carry on their branches the words of those who have wandered there and moanings that no human being could hear. The forests forget about the words and the snow covers them up when it coats each branch. This makes the new leaves of spring. The forgotten words have lost their meaning. Those who spoke them have died or gone astray. Sometimes they remain in the forests for the rest of their lives and no one knows what has become of them any more.

You, though, continue on your way. I hear your strange chant, so faint that anyone might think you were addressing the earth, praying softly to it.

Your father is that man walking toward the river. He's still gripping his childhood knife in his hand. He knows nothing of time on the roads nor of other countries. He's never had a taste for distant elsewheres.

He walks along, his head still stiff with his thoughts from the morning. Like everyone here, his days are ordered and there's just enough room left for a person to ask whether they'll visit the Café in the evening or whether they'll go straight home. And today he realises that it's a life of nothing. He pays no attention to what he passes. His steps lead him to the river and he lets them get on with it. In his pocket the old piece of paper is like soft skin beneath his fingers. He walks the way someone goes to war.

Everyone in the village knows the river. Children are kept away from it from a very early age with stories that he also heard. No one ever told them to your mother, though, and she didn't know that the river is full of sinkholes where the water churns, seething basins that drag the incautious down by the hair. People content themselves with being reminded that the river is there, close by, because all at once the murmur of the water reaches their ears. That's enough for them to move away from it. Sometimes they can't actually hear the noise. It's treacherous. A person has to be on their guard. Around here no one trusts water that doesn't stay where it is.

In the grand old days of the sawmill no one heard anything and they said that was the reason children would drown. The fathers would go back to work the next day all the same. It was fate. The river was the peril of the village. And people told themselves that every place has its peril. Death has to be feared. In one way or another. It's better to make it happen young. That puts a value on everyday life, even if it's low.

Your father is the man who's walking, searching his mind for the stories his mother told him as a child to keep him away from the river. Fears and fears...

On the same day, all morning your grandmother goes from farm to farm. She takes her time; for the return she'll need her strength to carry the full baskets. During her rounds each week she feels fully alive. As long as she can still do it, things will be fine.

In her head is the list of what she needs. It's the only way to take care of a family. Prepare what will be put on the table. She draws on everything she's learned in her life to take what doesn't cost too much and make it appetising. She chooses the herbs for each dish. Herbs are all that she grows. At times no one notices but she's on the lookout, she's tried a new flavour. If you both eat more slowly, she knows you're savouring it. She says to herself that at the same moment all three of you have the same taste in your mouths. At bottom, that's what family is. First of all that. That's what she learned when she was still small. Your mother also showed her how to bravely mix tart and sweet.

She still does it sometimes, it's her way of letting you know that she hasn't forgotten her. On those days you eat with particular relish.

Your grandmother has learned to drive anything she cannot solve out of her head. When thoughts come and nag at her, she sings to herself. And what is strange is that she's freed her mind by driving out God. If she still goes to church every Sunday it's because she's learned that in the village it's the only way to go unnoticed.

She never remembers her images from the night, but in the daytime – then she dreams. In the house she allows her gaze to linger on a piece of fabric, a tea towel, an apron with faded colours. Especially in shades of blue, dull, washed out. She enters into the colour and lets herself be carried along. She can dream for a long time, on her feet, eyes open. When she does her rounds outside in the open air, she dreams in a different way. It's childhood that comes to find her. She's taken those paths so many times she knows them by heart. She recovers her step of a little girl.

Today, it felt strange to her to have left your father sleeping in the house. He never sleeps that long. She knew very well that he'd had too much to drink the previous evening. She was afraid he'd start shouting again. She's so tired of the shouting. She had thought that once your mother left, the shouting would stop and everything would go back the way it was. But no. Your mother left anger in his body, and for that nothing can be done, she knows, she's seen enough of men from close up to learn it. She sometimes tells herself that if she'd managed to love that woman, everything would have settled down in time. But there it is. You she loves, yes, it's a matter of blood, the same blood that runs in her veins and yours, but she never was able to love your mother. She was a stranger, always a stranger. A woman of the roads and of another language. She was always a little afraid of her.

She sighs. In a sharp tone she quiets the dog at the first farm. It can't be helped, that dog never knows her right away. While it's barking, she's another stranger to it. Now it sniffs at her legs, recognises her smell. The farmer's wife is already at the door. They say hello. Your grandmother is once again the old woman that everyone knows. For the first time she wonders what it means to always be a stranger in the place where you live.

As for you, you've been walking for a long time, the dog at your side. Nothing could distract you. The house with the mist, the house with the hollow have disappeared perhaps behind your back, like your mother. You do not turn around. You wait for something to come up along the way, you don't know what, that will light your path.

I see that your steps are tired. No doubt it would be more sensible to go back to your own house, to the village, but something draws you further away. This day is a day for discovery. Your back against a tree, you let yourself slip to the ground.

Head raised, you try to understand. It may be a very long path.

You wonder where to go now. The world is so huge and your legs so slight. You remain squatting, your head against the smooth bark. Your body feels all numb.

You are leaning back against absence.

Every one of your days will lean back against absence. You are learning that no door will be able to open or close it.

You scrape at the earth with your fingertips. You recognise the damp earth by the river. You must have found yourself close to it. You plunge your whole hand into the soil, which does not resist. Then you move your fingers gently, one by one. The earth sticks to your skin.

You ought to go down to the river, put your hand in and let the water flow slowly over everything that will never be seen again. But.

With the tip of your finger you trace letters. You know the words of love in your mother's language and you can write them in silence. You press up against the mystery of that which disappears.

There are things that can only be understood when all light has yielded. All hope of light. When there's nothing left but the naked truth of bodies that go away forever and that will never be touched again. You learn all that in your flesh. And that means learning that your own body will also disappear one day. That the trees will remain, the river will remain, and perhaps too what you write here, with the tip of your finger, if no one, ever, erases your letters beneath their feet.

The words of unknown languages remain safe from mouths. No one hears them. Those words are the only ones that hold some life-bringing thing. Still. And that enter into the daylight. For it's truly necessary that all night cease.

The letters you trace do not need your eyes. You feel them with your fingertips. In the damp shade by the river you talk to your mother. Her untamed language is in you for all time. And always it's only your little life on this earth.

In your bones you have the ancient times of those who walk for others, who protect dreams.

Your father too is near the river. What he is hearing now is a voice that has come from his own childhood. That of your grandmother, calling him as evening falls. He was in the lodge, meticulously whittling the branches and decorating them with strange letters. His mother stood on the threshold of the house, cupping her mouth with her hands to project her voice. He let her call. His name, launched into the evening air, was a strange pleasure, he remembers. He existed more firmly in his mother's call. In that voice hailing him through the dusk. Much more than when he was present in front of her.

Today he's a man. In his memory he can still hear his name in the evening air. Right here, now, he would so much like to be called again in that special way used for calling children. He would go at once. Relieved of all that has passed through his mind since morning. Rid of that strange state he doesn't understand.

But there's nothing.

Only the slithering sound of the river. His pace slows.

What if he goes there, right down to the edge. His heart pounds. He breathes like someone tracking an animal. Why not go all the way to the end? What is there to be afraid of? Clear flowing water? But it's no use naming things calmly with words, his legs feel the weight of the fear. Fear of the river rises through the damp earth. As powerfully as when he was little and your grandmother, exasperated, would say If you keep that up the river will come and carry you away.

He walks on with measured steps. The vegetation changes closer to the water. He recognises plants that only grow in this shaded earth. Some are strange, with almost no stalk, their colours laid out directly upon the earth. He avoids trampling them, fixes his gaze on the patches of colour. He sees again the skirt with the indistinct pattern, the one your mother was wearing when she left. The usual clothes of other women, on her seemed odd. Her body didn't look the way it should when she wore them. Even when they were bought for her they looked as if they'd been borrowed from someone else. She left them in the closet and put her old skirt back on.

He says to himself that she wasn't made for buttons and fastenings. Her movements needed to be free, beneath light fabrics. Her legs needed more room. Here everything weighed her down.

And his body – was it light enough upon her? Every night that vigour that few men experience. Every night with her, the renewed pact of skins that seek each other, are drawn to one another. Why had he not felt anything special the last time, the last night? why had his body not given him any sign? does something under the skin not know such things? do bodies not know they're going to be separated for ever? how is it possible there should be nothing, nothing to indicate that the morning will be empty, and all other mornings empty.

He sees an animal creeping down toward the river and he makes a childlike move to try and catch it. The animal gets away.

He has the hard look of those who have lost everything in a single moment. The look of those who no longer have any hope. Saints can be made with a look like that. Or murderers. But him – he remains a man like any other. No war no cause will let him give form to what is struggling within him. Are the lives of some really worth the lives of others? Is he worth his own life now.

His heavy shoe has just crushed something. He doesn't stop. He heard the breaking sound more than he felt it. Something shatters beneath his feet, like glass, or ancient bones. And now he is seized by rage and the desire to trample on the bones of that woman, wherever she might be, and he's ashamed of his desire. Horrified at having thought it. He's afraid of himself. He has always wondered if the buried dead migrate silently under the earth and go down to the river to vanish.

Do the images of death that a person carries cause those who get too close to you to die?

Today he's sure that that woman, who his body still calls to, also had images of death beneath her skin. When they were in each other's arms, was that what they shared? Women of the roads like her could assimilate everything. Their bodies took the darkness of visions and rid themselves of it by scattering it along the roads. She, though, was no longer travelling. He had pinned her down in a home. She was no longer able to deliver herself of the images.

Had she disappeared because the images were weighing too heavily?

He arrives at the river. It's the first time he has gazed at it.

Today your grandmother hesitates before going on to the house of Émilienne, her old friend, as she always does at the end of her rounds. She doesn't know why. Her step is suspended.

What is coming back to her is the hopscotch game from her childhood. She sees it again, drawn in chalk on this same road. The earth was below and the sky above. The player hopped from one square to another and the world was in order. If anyone came a cropper it was because they couldn't keep their balance. It was just a matter of learning how. The order of the world was unchanging.

The memory comes back beneath her stiff, old woman's footsteps of today. She remembers. She was so young, she was still considered a child even though her breasts were growing. The boys had just begun to look at her. She could still play with the others. But she knew that soon her mother would keep her at home and that that would be the end of games.

And God had allowed to happen all that happened one summer's day, on that same road, on the flat world of the hopscotch. God had also been flattened. He had not resisted the man's heavy steps, or his immense hands. The hopscotch had. While her, she continued to hum as if she didn't feel the man's hands on her body, as if it was all taking place far, far away from her. She went on hopping from one square to the next. She hadn't been able to withstand, crushed beneath the pitiless weight of the man. Her body no longer felt anything. The mixed smells of tobacco and earth did not enter her nostrils. Her eyes were closed. Forget the face. Forget everything. When the man left her, she got back up, quickly. She erased every line of the hopscotch, rubbing away like a crazy person. God had been wiped away with the chalk. Beneath her feet of a little girl.

A person might believe they've wiped everything away, and go on with their life as if nothing were wrong. But no. One day, it's all there anew. And it's today.

Women like her do not set out on the roads. Yet that is what would have saved her. To go, leave everything, never see her house or her village again. A new life would have been needed for her herself to also be new again. But when a girl is from the village she stays in the village and she keeps her mouth shut and she runs into the man as he's coming out of the Café, he doesn't so much as look at her, and she says nothing. She forgets. The time comes when the girl asks herself if it actually even happened.

This morning, your grandmother knows that it really did happen. It was here, under her old woman's feet, and she, who never cries, sheds tears for the little girl she used to be. Today she realises she has spent her life suspended between sky and earth, humming with the flies and the bees. She no longer raises her eyes except to watch the slow and lovely journeys of the clouds. And if she goes to church, she no longer does anything there. Neither truly prays, nor takes communion. How can anyone commune with something that has fled?

This morning her little girl's step has come back into her feet. But it's with all her old woman's strength that she crushes in her memory the heavy body of the man, that she takes out a knife, sticks the blade into his belly, watches the blood flow, and the rattling sound the man makes is the death rattle. At last. Today, yes, she would kill him without any hesitation, she knows it, and all the way to her bones she feels an untamed delight.

You, the child, you've walked all the way to the water's edge and I'm afraid you'll misstep, because my hand cannot guide you. I can no longer see the dog by you. Your gaze is lost in the swirling water.

You remember. One day your father's shouting had made the air tremble more than usual in the house and his man's hand had come down again on your mother's cheek. All at once your heart was bursting in your chest. Your mother had frozen. Her whole life held tight in her clenched fists. She turned around abruptly and saw you. In her hand closing around yours, fury. Through the open door behind the two of you, you could hear your father's voice Where do you think you're going? but he didn't stop you. She was walking like someone who knows where they're going, who has merely delayed too long the moment of departure. She remained silent all along the way but you, you understood every-thing. You knew that the hand descending on her face had swept away the fragrant soup, the warmth of the stove in winter, and the softness of the bed. All of that had to be finished with and you, you were prepared to go with her. You gripped her hand tightly. Nothing would have stopped you. You could leave, both of you. Run away to the ends of the earth. Run away. Your heart was a war drum.

She had stopped where you are now, facing the river. She stood there. Who knew what the next step might be? In your head there was no longer anything but a large empty space so your mother could spin some more. But she didn't move. Then she gave a big sigh and let go of you. You clutched her skirt firmly in your fingers. She took a step toward the river. You clung to the fabric. Your whole child's body braced. You stopped her.

Today, once more you see her face as she turned toward you. Her face of that day. Drained of everything, stamped only with her infinite love for you. That face will go with you throughout the rest of your life. Hold onto it inside you and forget all the rest. You'll find it again in the face of every Madonna in paintings. Hold onto it. You – you know that mothers who have that face are those who one day were able to hold back their step. A child understands everything.

The step backwards was the step of your life. Because you would have followed her. While she – she knew it.

She sat down on the river bank, held you tight against her. She continued to look at you, you studied her face and she spoke to you, for a long time, as she'd never spoken before.

To begin with you found it hard to understand. She was telling you that there is a house. The steep house. That before taking big decisions in life, a person has to climb up there. She inhabited her words and you followed her.

Today your memory leads you into your mother's mouth. You follow afresh each of the words to the secret of her mouth. She was saying.

You'll see, every room goes straight up. No furniture can be in it. You live there sitting on the ground or on your knees. If you get up and walk you have to spread your arms to keep your balance. It's a house where no one can shout or make sudden movements. You're much too busy with every step. Shouting could make the air shake too hard against the walls, and the stones wouldn't be able to resist.

The steep house is a wise house. Living at the top of a cliff calms the mind.

She added One day you'll find it. It's there, it's waiting for you. Each of us has our steep house deep inside. But most people are too afraid to climb up there. You, you'll have to do it.

Your mother's index finger passed back and forth across your forehead. She was smoothing your father's shouts in your head of a child, wiping away finger by finger the hand that strikes, and gradually the terrifying things pulled back, lost their power to make you smaller. She was making room for the steep house in your head. You remember how you pressed against her. You offered her your face, eyes shut. When she caressed it with her so precise fingers, it was as if she were drawing it in the air and that having a face became easy.

I'd like to pass my index finger across your forehead today and bring back the infinite trust that made your heart swell at each of her words.

She went on You'll see, if you go in and you manage to climb up to the second floor, all the way to the top, and even higher, to the little turret, in the distance you'll see a town. The town belongs only to those who dare to climb as far as there, and it will be your town. You'll see it far away and you won't know if you're looking at houses or boats, bell towers or masts with their sails furled. No one actually knows. In front will be the ocean. You'll see how huge the ocean is but at first it'll be like a mist bordering the town... You listened. Your father's shouting was being wiped away. Nothing could resist your mother's voice. Nothing.

Since then you've tried to join up the words boat, ocean, and mast, but you only know the forest and the river. No image came from the words put together in your head. Nothing. Until today your steep house has remained lurking deep inside you.

Today is the day when you can reach it. You feel it rising in you, coming from a space deep inside that you do not know, that had been waiting. Eyes closed, you see it behind your eyelids. It rises up in front of you. And you enter it. I follow you, stepping soundlessly. By some miracle you remain on your feet but your mother was right, everything rises straight up. You can no longer think of anything but your foot-steps, one after another. Nothing else.

Your fear slips from your heart into your legs: you have to keep your whole body in balance. Too much one way or the other and the house could collapse.

You have to move forward with even steps. Like a tightrope walker. Had your mother been able to climb all the way up to the top of her turret? You think to yourself that for you it's easier since you don't weigh heavily on the earth.

Your feet barely rest on each step. You look at the ancient knots in the grain of the wood and in them you see the hands of your grandmother. In other places the wood seems never to have been touched. It's smooth, with a beautiful warm colour. Then it's your mother's hands that you see. You're carried along gently by the hands of the two women. You cannot fall. I see you slowly mounting each step higher and still higher. All the way to the turret.

The staircase has so many steps that they shouldn't be counted. You feel the fresh air coming to meet your face. You must keep climbing. Without fear. I hold you in my gaze.

The house murmurs like the forest or like the water in the river. You let the sound enfold you. You keep going.

Now the wind is blowing hard. You no

longer have the faded red fabric of her dress to cling to. You have nothing to hold you up now but the air. So you find a far-off point, the way she did, and you lash your gaze to it. She told you that in the distance your town would appear.

You wait.

You see nothing.

Was your mother truly a crazy vagabond who spouted nonsense, as your father still sometimes shouts?

With all your strength you reaffirm your trust in the words she uttered. You drive away all the insults and all the doubts.

You see her again as you alone were able to see her.

I hold you in my gaze. I do not leave you. As long as you are up aheight I'm there. I wait with you. The wind is stinging your eyes more and more, there, behind your eyelids. I feel it too.

And now the returned face of your mother, her face of infinite love, at last opens the horizon. Your tears flow and you do nothing to stop them.

It's through the tears that you see.

First the mist. The sky no longer has any known colour. It's a sky that knows neither light nor nighttime. You'd need to touch it to feel the new colour, but it's not possible to touch the sky. You accept the unknownness of this sky. And finally your town appears.

Your face now is the face of a child no longer afraid of anything. You see the town inside you. It reveals itself. Its rooftops are high and they reflect slow regular motions like the beating of your heart. Your heart beats in unison with the slow heart of the town. You let your gaze discover the ocean.

There.

Your mother had said that the ocean bordered the town and it is there, but you understand the landscape differently. It's the town that borders the ocean. It was built to give a border to something that has none, because men like your father, like all those from villages, need limits. Your mother, on the other hand, did not. And you?

You feel that which has no end quivering inside you.

You lift your hand up high. Your fingers flutter toward the sky. You feel the wind on your palm. It isn't the same as the wind that blows in the forest. It's fresh and humid, salty. You slowly lower your hand till it's right in front of your face and you lick the wind that's left on your fingers. Now, in your mouth your mother's words find their way briskly. She had said masts and boats. They're there, behind the houses and the alleyways of the town. They're in your mouth and you say the words with the salty taste of the wind. It's a different world that you are drawing and you like this world.

For a long time you stay like that in front of your town and the ocean. You feel that in your body new things are seeking to take their place.

Your father has let his legs bend at the river's edge. He's on his knees, the knife in his hand.

A very old fear has come back into his mind. As a little boy at school, when he learned that in the distant past humans did not stand upright to face the world but were on all fours like the animals, an ancient, baseless fear gripped him. His teacher's words entered directly into his bones and for the first time he felt his skeleton, beneath all his muscles and his skin, the skeleton that kept him seated or standing. He had never thought about it before. At the same time, the image of all the people from the village on their hands and knees like humans at the start of time had taken hold of him, and it was dizzying. No part of their lives was possible any longer. Was that all it took? let the skeleton resume its former posture, and none of the life they knew was possible any more? So that was all that mattered in the case of humans. They were vertical or not. A matter of bones and joints.

Some part of his confidence in the strength of the world had failed. He had not been able to talk about it when he went home. Who would have understood? He watched his mother going about her tasks in the house, imagined her too bent down, and none of her motions fit any more in the space of the kitchen. Nor in his head. He watched his father and couldn't help imagining him on all fours also. That hurt him. He was ashamed, and afraid that he too would one day find himself like an animal. No longer human.

He had straightened his posture. It made his mother and his father proud when he held himself erect. If they'd only known the reason for that straight back. Whenever he felt himself slouch, a dizziness in his bones would come over him. Later he kept the habit of holding his neck stiff, no longer knowing where it came from.

Today his old mother is stooped. Soon she will rejoin the earth. As for him, no one has ever known how he struggled so as to never ever be a man on his knees.

When he first met your mother, that

woman who walked so proudly and silently, it was as if she didn't come from the lineage of those who at the beginning stared at the earth. She held herself straight, and the suppleness of her hips suggested that it cost her no effort. Her gaze travelled far in front of her. She carried her eyes high. She seemed an outsider among all those they knew and that was what he had loved. Her, he had never imagined bent toward the earth. That was not possible. And with her, there would never be any risk of returning to a stooped life. She held him upright in her gaze.

That power was as great as the power of her naked body pressing against his every night. Perhaps even greater.

But a person cannot entrust their bones to someone else. That's too much. He had resented her for exactly that which he desired most deeply. To entrust to someone else the power to stay upright, that was too much, yes, by far. So gradually he had been overcome by the fury of being dependent and not even understanding what he was dependent on. He had believed that his desire for her was the simple kind of desire that causes bodies to tremble and makes the space of a single night so powerful, but today he reckons that desire was much vaster. Was infinite. That the desire touched on things that went far beyond what is called love; or perhaps that alone, that is what love is? He no longer has any idea.

She disappeared. Was he too heavy to carry?

People could say whatever they wanted about her disappearance. Him, he knew for certain she would never have abandoned you to go walk the roads. She would have taken you with her. In her strange way. The woman who didn't know how to take her child's hand the way mothers do in these parts. Who did not have in her arms the weight of children being held against the chest and rocked. She carried you in her gaze and you always followed her. You were of the same blood as her. Both of you were free. Not him.

Your father is not a father. He feels it and has always felt it. Perhaps he could have been the father of a child brought up in the ways of the village. Not of the child that you are. He can't do it. He can't think 'my child'. You, this child who doesn't talk, doesn't ask for anything, he prefers not to think you.

Today he is on his knees before the river. He's looking at the earth. Like all those of his species long before him. Those who have understood that the sky is not for them.

This man on his knees smells the warm scent of the shaded earth. He fills his chest with it. It's a living scent.

And now he sees the back of the woman walking before him in the town where the fair was held, where his destiny was formed. It's all there. Brought back by the mingled smell of earth and water. Himself, taken away from the noisy crowd, led to a grove of trees, following her blindly. Literally abducted. Removed from the known world. All of his being gathered in his body, which in a single moment he was finally inhabiting. Entirely and without any fear.

A blessing. The most beautiful moment of his whole life. Those few steps. Willing ones. Far from the world. All his life was contained there. Between a marketplace and some trees. Life can sometimes be contained in the mere space of a few steps. What of it.

Your grandmother has reached the end of her rounds, she doesn't know how. Sometimes the body takes charge and that's fine. Her steps have led her to Émilienne's, despite everything. Her last stop.

She says as she does each time, I've come to your place last for the eggs. To make sure they're on top in the basket. And Émilienne replies, I set them aside for you. Nice fresh ones.

It's a ritual. Émilienne then counts the eggs, which she places, well wrapped, on the top of the basket. Then she opens the dresser and takes out cups. It's either a herbal tea or a liqueur, both home-made; it depends on their mood.

Both of them have spent their whole lives here. Émilienne lives in the last house in the village. After that it's the road. She likes being at the edge. In other times people would surely have said she was a witch.

Together, they no longer have any need of remembering.

They know. It's a kind of rest.

They drink calmly, like two quiet old ladies, by a window, in a village. But truly, there is no calm. Not even here, where nothing they do not already know can cross their path. There is no peace.

Émilienne has gotten up. In the same dresser where she keeps the glasses, she opens a drawer. She takes out a small box that she places in front of your grandmother.

Your grandmother raises her eyes but Émilienne has already turned away, she's watching the road through the window, lets your grandmother open the box without saying anything to her. Now your grandmother is holding a strip of red cloth embroidered with old beads. Of course she recognises it right away.

Where did you get this?

Her old friend comes back and sits down again. She first finishes her bitter-tasting liqueur and puts her glass down softly. Then she speaks.

She used to come here sometimes, like you. She'd say nothing, or almost nothing. She would lean on the windowsill and watch the road. The road, for sure that was what drew her. I can understand that.

The child? Did she talk to you about the child? Did she bring him with her?

No. She always came alone.

A great sense of relief in your grand-mother's heart. She sees your mother. A woman around whom love revolved without managing to take root. Holding the bracelet in her hand, she sees the day when your father came back with her, there, her long skirt that moved at every step, her skin scrubbed by the rain and sun of the roads. What madness was that? And her silence. Not one word. The only time her voice was heard was when she sang. Songs of the road, since she didn't have her own country. Husky, rhythmic sounds that softened at times, giving the listener a chill. Your father would tell her to keep quiet. So she would. Entirely. Then he started to shout. She no longer recognised her son. He frightened her.

She remembers that when your mother's belly grew big she had thought everything would go back to normal but she hadn't counted on the power of the road. Your mother always had to be going out, and that drove your father crazy. And then she had started taking you into the forest. He didn't want her muddling your head with her language and her stories from no place. So she would run away with you into the forest.

And you – you copied her. You didn't talk.

Today your grandmother looks at the bracelet, sewn with small light stitches like threads of snow. Yes, she recognises it without a doubt.

This old woman has taught you everything you need to know to be able to live in the village like the others. She taught you to be leery of the river, to recognise whether a dog can be approached or not, how to eat things that are from around here, and how to make other people forget you're there. When she gives you advice you continue to do whatever you were doing, so it looks as if you didn't hear anything. But she's realised that this is your way of listening. The words enter into a corner of your head. You remember everything. Absolutely everything. And she wouldn't have liked anyone else in the village to teach you anything at all. Even Émilienne.

Why did your mother use to come all this way?

She gets up. There are days when nothing happens in the regular way. Who knows why. Her son sleeping late in the house. Her finding herself with the bracelet in her hand. All at once she feels a pang in her heart. What about you?

From holding your mother's bracelet, she hears a silent alert. She's at the door.

Don't you want to know what she said to me when she gave me the bracelet?

No. Then in an outbreath she adds What she said she said to you, right? Not to me. So.

She leaves without looking back. No, she doesn't want to know anything. She must get back, must find you, you, the child. She's in a hurry. Something is on its way again and she doesn't know what. Why dear God why.

She takes rapid steps. Her load is heavy but she moves along. As she's passing the church, of a sudden she stops. Putting her two baskets down abruptly, she stands in front of the doorway. Her heart is thumping.

She never goes in aside from Sundays. Never alone. This time he's going to listen to her! She leaves her baskets and enters. She holds herself straight, does not kneel down. And her voice is clear and sharp when she says You let things be done to me that even animals don't do. And my heart closed up. I raised my son with a heart filled with fear. And that is not good at all. So I'm telling you. The only good thing left to me is the child. And I don't care a bit if he's not like the others. If anything at all happens to him, I'll come back to this church of yours and burn the damn place down.

Your grandmother hastens toward the house. In her step she has the strength of those that evil has not beaten down. She says to herself that she will save you, whatever happens. From anything.

The dog has disappeared now.

You look at me, and in your eyes I recognise the mute expectation of the child I used to be. Your gaze is the gaze that stunned me one night. It was in a dream. I was there, sitting, alone, I was six or seven years old and I was watching myself, the woman I had become. There was such expectation in my gaze of a child that I woke up. Moved deeply. And I wrote. It was the dog from my childhood that led you. It's the breath of my childhood that swells your chest. We are together.

It could be that at the top of the tower in the steep house we stay for a long time now, contemplating uncertain things.

There is no longer anything in our heads. The space is empty.

We've entered the territory of doubt in the world. Nothing is delimited any more. Each thing can become a world. There's no longer anything that can be confidently named. Even the alphabet has become a series of outlines, each letter an outline and a world unto itself. Naturally, we sense the dull fear that is trying to hold us back. When someone sets aside the naming of the world so as to allow something to happen, can it be returned to later? Or do they have to disappear, in madness, in the river? Where can they find the vast confidence needed to undertake the venture?

The steep house is demanding.

We hesitate before the unknown inside ourselves. Since the disappearance of our mother, confidence does not come easily. We no longer have anything but our childhood to guide us. We are at the very top of ourselves.

Clinging to one moment, then the next, the way our fingers gripped the dog's fur. Holding on to the present. Nothing but the present. With all our strength. Nothing before. Nothing after. We mustn't want to know anything. Keep anything but emptiness in our heads. We mustn't think. We mustn't think. Mustn't ask ourselves if one day we'll be able to go back to the calm world of named things. We must dare.

We wait for something to come from the ocean or the town. We're ready.

It could be that the father's belly is now pressed against the earth. His head is right by the water. A person would need to lean down to hear what he's murmuring. A song learned in school a long, very long time ago. A song telling of a bird that flies far away. Between his mouth and the earth there is so little space. His lips brush against the grass. He reaches out his hand and lets it hang above the water. The tips of his fingers touch the river. Then he buries his other hand in the earth and he weeps.

It could be that this man at the river's edge is thinking of the water as a deliverance. He clutches his childhood knife in his hand. The earth sticking to his fingers gives the handle of the knife an almost warm feeling. It could be that he's thinking of the heat of blood.

Stand up! Inside his head the always slightly husky voice of his wife might say Stand up! He would never have heard her say those words but there, in front of the briskly flowing water, there would be no doubt.

Standing, facing the river, he might take the drawing out of his pocket. In a movement that nothing in the preceding seconds would have allowed us to expect, he would throw the piece of paper into the river. He would remain there unmoving, stunned by what he himself has done. As if this irrevocable act did not truly belong to the man he is. As if this gesture revealed a determination that he does not recognise.

He would close the knife slowly, put it back in his pocket.

We know for certain that he will again touch his childhood with the tips of his earth-stained fingers buried in his pocket. He will continue to feel its warmth. For a long time.

But for the moment, he would watch the piece of paper gradually disappear, first becoming soaked by the water and, made heavy, slipping just below the surface, as they say, then the ink washes off and the paper, as if relieved of its indecipherable message, suddenly gathers speed, that of the water moving rapidly away. Toward what? The question would arise in his mind for the first time. Yes, toward what? What larger waterway, what sea was waiting for the river from the village at the end of its way? The thought of the place where the water of the river mingled with other water would make something new in his head. A different space. Unknown. Linked by the unfolded paper, that perhaps by now has been washed clean.

It could be that in a brief flash the man sees the body of his wife. Alive. Perfect.

Once again he feels his sex standing up. The river flows on at his feet. His hand lets go of the knife so as to reach the part of him that is upright, useless, and yet. And as if this motion too could not have belonged to him a few seconds earlier, beneath his fingers he feels the delicate, quivering skin of his own sex. It's to his naked wife, there in front of him in his memory, that he offers every pulse of his blood, entirely concentrated in that part of him which nothing was calling to pleasure any more. He feels the thrum of the river's moist earth rising from the soles of his feet all the way to his belly, and in a long breath he offers his pleasure to the murmuring water.

It could be that from the threshold of the house, your grandmother calls and calls you in the evening, her hands cupped around her mouth. She would remember the time when she used to call her own son in the fading light. Today she would be calling her son's child, because it's what she has always done and because it's in such a way that things ought to resume their accustomed places. And so for a long time, as she sits on the bench outside the house, silences would be interspersed with your name sent out into the air.

Does a name travel long after all voices have fallen quiet? do the low branches of the trees carry it all the way to their crowns so the name, borne on the wind, tenderly, like a little one in the mouth of its mother, can see the vastness of the forest canopy. How much time does it take for a name to drop back down and reach the ear of the one being named?

It could be that she takes the bracelet with the old beads out of the pocket of her apron. Slips it gently onto her wrist. Is that what the mother of the child would have wanted? Is it her job to wear it now? She would move her fingers slowly over the beads and feel the fatigue of all the steps she never dared to take beyond the village.

She would remember the bold gait of that woman, who she had never been able to put her arms around. See again her long slim hands. Look at her own hands, worn by the work she does every day, it isn't the same thing. The hands of the village women do things that no one notices because nothing seems to be created from their actions. They make the wellbeing of houses, nothing more, and that cannot be seen.

The bracelet on her wrist now – that would be something different. It would give her dreams.

She would say to herself that she ought to have shown the woman what her son had been able to do with tree branches when he was little. Why, for all these years, had she forgotten about the beauty that came from her little one's hands? Why had she forgotten her motherly wonder at the first thing her son made? His tree branches that served no purpose. Just that of beauty. Why had the son become this sorrowful adult who couldn't cope any more, who drank at the Café who shouted whose neck was held stiffer and stiffer before collapsing? It could be that her fingers slowly stroke the beads of the bracelet.

We hear her calls, rolling around each of the beads sewn onto the bracelet. The son hears them too.

In those calls he would hear two contradictory things. Come back and leave. Come back so as to leave. Truly. Is that not what the woman he had chosen to bring back home had been showing him all those years? One day, it's necessary to leave. And never mind the village and the people who'll say He's mad. He would carry his work with him at his fingertips. A few tools in his bag and the road in front of him. Wasn't that what he envied in the woman?

That freedom, which he wanted so much and which she had in her blood?

Was it necessary to have kept her in the confined space of the village? Was it necessary for her to disappear? Was all the anger and the bad wine necessary?

He'll be afraid to say goodbye.

He'll leave the way she did. Like a thief. A thief of what? of the pain that's caused? Does the person who leaves always have to feel they've stolen something? A little freedom in this world, a deeper breath of air – is that wanting too much? He is the one whose breath has been stolen for too long.

All his life he'll have accepted the law of the village and of time. All his life he's been afraid, in a part of him that had no name. Afraid, if he did not agree, did not submit, of becoming once again like the men from the times of stooping. From before there was language among humans. A man who doesn't look at the horizon, who doesn't look into another man's face. A man pinned to the ground by his eyes and a stooping spine. Was it in his mother's milk he'd drunk that?

Now he would walk toward the house and think of the Christ from his childhood, that was in the old church; even as a child he didn't like to look at him, that man who had suffered for him for all those who were there, kneeling before the divine pain, and those around the world who were kneeling too. He was straight on the cross, but that came at the cost of nails and blood while they – they were stooped, always stooped, no longer on all fours, true, but on their knees. To remind themselves that it wouldn't take much to go back to being men from before there were men? He hadn't asked, hadn't wanted, for a man to suffer for him, even if it was the son of a god. Those Sunday Masses were a torment. He already felt guilty. Guilty. Guilty. And all he could do was hold himself straight and accept, do what the others did. While the fear was there, dull and lurking. In his blood.

The one and only time he'd allowed his desire alone to keep him straight, were the few steps he had taken behind the woman in the faded skirt.

He wished he could find once again in his legs, in his back, the lightness of that so-short walk. The walk of his life. The walk of his desire, his, no one's but his.

He would know that then, he had been free. And that he'd resented her for having made him feel what freedom could be. He would know he should never have brought her back to the village. He should have left with her, gone far away. Taken to the roads. Let his pal drive the lorry back on his own. And never mind his mother's consternation and the gossip in the village. He'd have been free to dis-cover the world with the woman of his desire. He'd have been alive. But it hadn't even crossed his mind at the time. Not even crossed his mind!

We see his thoughts rapping at the tips of his fingers. We feel the buzz of his thoughts beneath his skin. He sees the whole of himself clearly. He sees that he was so stuck in the lime of days and nights all alike that he couldn't even have imagined anything else. The hidden bonds held him down more firmly than he could understand. He remained where his father and his father's father were buried, where his fiancée, who had died too young, was buried too. The strongest bonds are not always with the living. Fear is a good maker of bonds. The dead do the rest.

He sees that the woman of his desire carried her own dead in the folds of her skirt, and for that reason he would have had to let her stride along, the wind swelling her heart. Her own dead were free too. She didn't keep them enclosed in her two hands joined in prayer. Her dead were able to fly over the treetops, in the brightness of daybreak, or instead lose themselves even further away beyond heavens and hells, higher and further than the sky that can be seen by the eyes of man and woman, in a space where everything is transformed and becomes something else, and yet still belongs to life. Yes, her dead were free in their journey. And that truly was how life should be lived. She didn't keep anything. Her presence was impossible in the village because she was at peace with losing everything, even her dead. Today he would know that that is what it means to live.

And he – he has not lived.

We are no longer afraid now. The images are there. Voices and faces come to life in our heads. We imagine.

The reality of the world does not lose anything by it. Quite the opposite. We remember the open palms of our mother's hands, and all we saw in them that was unknown and lovely. We understand that the Never again does not take that away, that there, there are treasures for our whole life. That will not disappear.

We can even manage to say to ourselves that our mother is dead. Such a reality is no longer impossible. We know that we will never see her again but that we shall be able to imagine her. We have the power to face up to it. We'll be able to let her face come back, summoned by any other thing. The colour of a sky will enable it, or the curve of a hip in a painting. We'll no longer be afraid of losing her again and again. And of our being no more than a lost child.

Our dreaming is powerful. It is at work.

We are learning.

We find balance in each step we take. We can descend, one stair at a time, in the steep house. The door is still open. We are no longer afraid. We can climb back up there whenever we want.

We grow as we walk.

We learn that the bodies of mothers will never reappear again. Because mothers' bodies do not reappear. Ever. That's how it is. The bodies of mothers are erased from the bodies of the living. They become nothing. Nothingness. There remain only murmured words, gestures that seem as if slowed down, barely made. A breath. That is what a mother's body is.

Time labours to take its proper place in us. To delimit the nothingness of the mother. The nothingness asks for space. The place that had been empty. In this way living things take on a different form inside us. Out of respect for the nothingness. It has to be so. So we can live with our living body among the living.

In our solitary walk, that is what is at work. We sense the deep displacement. It comes from the earth and its tangled roots as they move aside to make room. Our voice is in harmony with that which has no name. The empty place of the mother is a lovely wellspring.

And as we walk we can at last imagine her leaving the village.

Leaving all of us.

Leaving me.

I have her gently close the door behind her, she who always left doors open despite the father's shouts Do you want just anyone to come walking into our house! On that morning, yes, she would have gently closed the door. So as to leave all of us to our lives where not just anyone came walking in. Perhaps she would say to herself that she had always been just anyone. Then I have her walk briskly, far in my gaze, far. She would not encounter anybody since it would barely be daybreak. She might perhaps be singing.

Little by little she would become a dot far away from the village, at the edge of an indistinct stretch of water. Clouds or a light mist would soften all colours. She would look into the distance then simply at her feet. Feet that had walked for a long time on roads, that were worn by the weather rubbing against the skin. Her feet would have a long history. This history would rise, clinging to her ankles like a climbing plant, making its way up her legs as far as her chest. She would have seen so many lives passing in the palms of men and women who crossed her path. She would be marked with so many passions so many sorrows. When her feet bore her right to the water, she would wash herself clean of it all.

Be new, never. She would know that no one can know life and be new. She would think in her language that she was the living mesh of everything she had encountered. A palimpsest. That respite was in the sky over her head, in the waves that carried her gently, that she would not return to the world of clothed people.

I imagine the mother's hard tears flowing far away, in the river, flowing to the big waterway and further further still, all the way to the place where there are no more banks.

I walk.

There is the time of clocks, that of the village, the time that passes since the disappearance of my mother and that can be counted. And then there's the other time, that which no one can see, a time in which the dead and the living are like the grass in the fields and the grass in gardens, similar and different. Separated by something than cannot be named. It's neither the colour, nor the walls of the gardens, nor the rocks that distinguishes them. Not even the attentions of gardeners. It's something else, that we feel deep inside and that makes the difference. One day, we've lived as much time without them as with them. The time of our childhood has been left behind.

It's clear that in the morning air the soft breath of those we love can be felt, even if they're dead, even if never again. This belongs to us and remains a secret.

I walk.

I imagine the house where I was born,

the house where my father was born, the house where my parents conceived me. It's strange. All these things that have happened in houses, rooms, roofs over heads and the changing light of different countries, shining here on a kitchen table, there on a garden in summer. I reflect on it. Like never before in this way, I think about time. The time from before my birth, then that of my coming into the world. Before me, my parents had a life. And their parents too. So it is with the world. How do lives follow on from one another? How does that happen? Then I say to myself, Since how long have there been days without my mother, and I'm able to count them.

I remember that it was an April day and that the spring had not yet properly arrived.

Today I walk along the shore of the ocean. I imagine beyond the story of the child.

Images come. They are free. And it's there, living in me. I sense the hum of the world calling me. Inside me there's room for every woman every man. For the ocean and for the mist. For the light that inches across the sand.

I accept that the world has toppled inside me without my knowing what awaits me. I feel. It's the adventure of my life. It engrosses me entirely.

I discover the silence inhabited by my own body, and it is a place in which to live.

The distance between the outside and the inside has been reduced: only skin, fragile, alive, letting the world through. A quivering. Inside, the intimate alchemy that makes images. What the world offers is inexhaustible and I understand that. Nothing remains but to give it my whole attention and wait for it to unfurl.

A powerful joy sweeps through me.

I learn that a human being has no limits, that it's enough to move away a little from the village, to accept the dizziness of the steep, and everything becomes possible. The imagination keeps madness at bay.

I learn the freedom of the river that reflects the world.

What I imagine is as true as reality. And it is my life. It's the peril of full freedom. I can face it because language is holding me firm.

I imagine.

For each of us.

So that the forgotten secret words should be recognised in each of us.

So as to find again, as in a dream, the silenced language, the language from before all other languages, that which has neither name nor country and belongs to us all.

January 20, 2016

Founded in 2014, **Les Fugitives** is an independent press publishing contemporary literary fiction and narrative non-fiction in translation from the French, as well as modern classics and contemporary English originals in 'the quick brown fox' collection.

In *the quick brown fox*:

No. 91/92: notes on a Parisian commute
by **Lauren Elkin**

We Still Have the Telephone
by **Erica Van Horn**

In translation from the French:

Eve out of Her Ruins and *The Living Days*
by **Ananda Devi**
trans. Jeffrey Zuckerman

This Tilting World
by **Colette Fellous**
trans. Sophie Lewis

Now, Now, Louison and *Nativity*
by **Jean Frémon**
trans. Cole Swensen

Translation as Transhumance
by **Mireille Gansel**
trans. Ros Schwartz

A Respectable Occupation
by **Julia Kerninon**
trans. Ruth Diver

Little Dancer Aged Fourteen
by **Camille Laurens**
trans. Willard Wood

Blue Self-Portrait and *Poetics of Work*
by **Noémi Lefebvre**
trans. Sophie Lewis

Suite for Barbara Loden and *The White Dress*
by **Nathalie Léger**
trans. Natasha Lehrer and Cécile Menon

Exposition
by **Nathalie Léger**
trans. Amanda DeMarco

The Governesses and *The Fool and Other
Moral Tales*
by **Anne Serre**
trans. Mark Hutchinson

Selfies
by **Sylvie Weil**
trans. Ros Schwartz

• www.lesfugitives.com •

• This first English-language edition published by Calypso Editions in the United States of America in April 2020 and by Les Fugitives in the United Kingdom in May 2022 • Les Fugitives Ltd, 91 Cholmley Gardens, Fortune Green Road, West Hampstead, London NW6 1UN • www.lesfugitives.com • Originally published as *L'enfant qui* © Actes Sud, 2017 • English-language translation © Bill Johnston, 2020 • Title page illustration and cover design by Sarah Schulte • Text design and typesetting by MacGuru Ltd •
A CIP catalogue record for this book is available from the British Library • The rights of Jeanne Benameur and Bill Johnston to be identified respectively as author and translator of this work have been identified in accordance with Section 77 of the Copyright, Designs and Patents Act 1988 • Printed in England by TJ Books, Padstow, Cornwall • ISBN 978-1-8384904-2-3 • Cet ouvrage a bénéficié du soutien du Programme d'aide à la publication de l'Institut français. • This book was awarded a Grant for the Arts by Arts Council England.